SIMON & SCHUSTER BOOKS FOR YOUNG READERS

Everything I Know About

CARS

A collection of made-up facts,
Educated Guesses, and Silly Pictures about
Cars, Trucks, and other Zoomy things

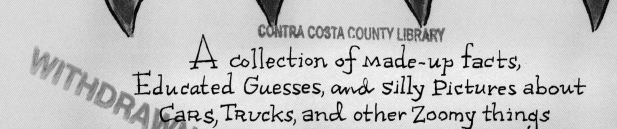

SUNROOF!

EASY TO PARK!

COOL HOOD ORNAMENT!

LICH-

TEN-

HELD

NEW YORK LONDON TORONTO SYDNEY

IDON'T KNOW MUCH ABOUT REAL CARS, but I'm an expert on made-up cars, so this book is a big traffic jam of mostly made-up cars.

Since this book is mostly made up, you should probably not use it as a repair manual when you and your friends get bored on a Saturday afternoon and decide to take apart your dad's new sport-utility vehicle. Also, this

Me in my made-up BEATNIK CAR

book will <u>not</u> explain why you have to ride around in a clunky old minivan while your best friend gets to zoom around listening to loud music in a fancy red sports car. So don't even ask.

MADE-UP CARS CAN DO ANYTHING!

Okay, those are the rules. Now let's go for a ride!

RED CARS are the FASTEST kind!

Prehistoric cave painting of cavemen trying to invent cars.

SINCE THE BEGINNING OF TIME, people have liked the idea of going fast while sitting on their butts, so there have been many attempts to invent cars.

It all started when prehistoric cavemen tried putting steering wheels on animals. The cavemen figured this would work because the animals already had car stuff on them, like horns and leather seats. Also, the animals already had cool car names like Impala and Jaguar. But it turned out that real impalas and jaguars don't like backside drivers. So it was back to the old drawing rock for the cavemen.

CAVEMEN HAD MUCH BETTER LUCK →
INVENTING THE "SKATEBONE."

AFEW YEARS LATER the Ancient Egyptians invented a dune buggy. But engines weren't invented yet, so their dune buggy had to be pulled by three guys in skirts. As you can imagine, these guys couldn't run very fast while wearing tight skirts, so their dune buggy was slow and boring. After a while they just left it out in the desert, where it was later discovered by a guy from Gurnee, Illinois, who turned it into a roller-coaster ride called the "Lost Lunch of King Tut."

Ancient Egyptian Steering Wheel

CARS WERE FINALLY INVENTED by two horses who got tired of carrying people around all the time. There were lots of humans trying to invent cars, but they could never figure out what kind of power to put into the engine. Meanwhile, these two horses put their own power into an engine and it worked great.

That's how horsepower was invented.

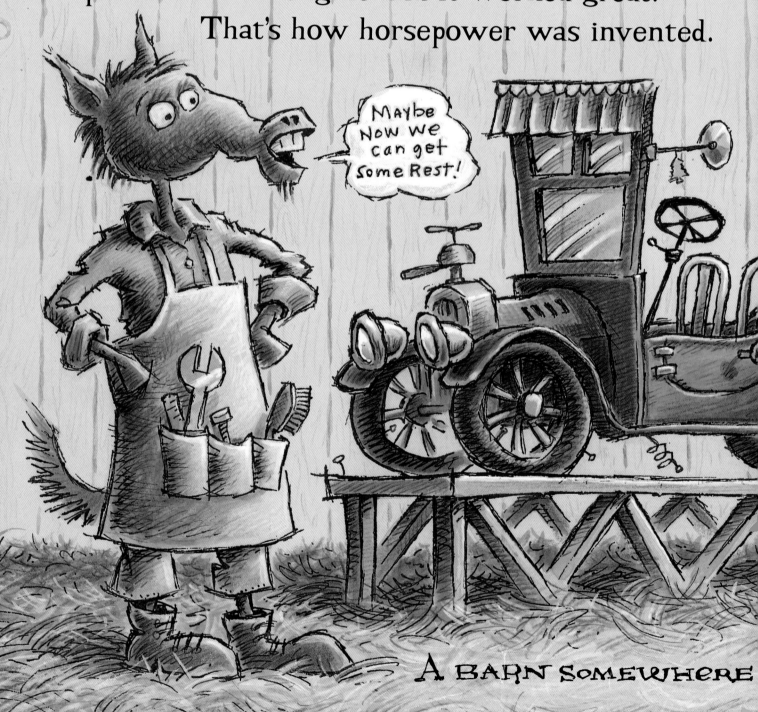

A BARN SOMEWHERE

Then some humans helped to finish the job by adding stinky exhaust fumes, fuzzy dice, and genuine Corinthian leather. The two horses weren't crazy about any of those things, so they got out of the car business. But to this day the term "horse sense" is used in honor of those horses, Winnie and Nay, who first invented the car.

IN OHIO ~ 1902

Limousine

NO BALL BOUNCING

BIRDS GOTTA FLY

Movie Stars like these cars; so do Real TALL People.

MOTOR* HOME

CAR POOL LANE

* SHOWN WITH OPTIONAL CAR POOL.

Cars

I COME IN ALL SHAPES AND SIZES. Some People Like BIG CARS and some People Like itty-bitty, teenie-weenie cars.

OH, Look, Honey! Isn't it Cute?!

NEW!

the MINI-VAN

SUN ROOF!

NO BARKING ZONE

CAUTION! CONTENTS UNDER PRESSURE. OPEN DOOR SLOWLY!

PRESSURE GUAGE

Room for 37 kids, 2 soccer Balls, 1 Football, 3 Bags of Groceries, 16 Spilled Juice Boxes, and 1 DOG

ANY CAR BOOK that's worth a darn has to have a cutaway view. So with some help from my Technical Advisor, Max, I cut a car in half and discovered that: 1. People get kind of uptight when their car is cut in half. 2. Cars are actually powered by wind.

MAX the MANIC MECHANIC

Here's how it works. First, wind comes into the front of the car, turning a fan, which makes the engine turn. Inside the engine are things called "jumpers" which jump up and down to make sparks. To keep all these sparks inside the engine, the holes in the engine are filled by special plugs called spark plugs. Next to the engine is a thing called

② AIR TURNS FAN

③ FAN TURNS ENGINE

BACK-UP SUPPLY OF TANGLED WIRES

① AIR ENTERS HERE

BOX OF GEARS

BRAKE SHOE

the alternator, which is what makes the engine alternate between working and not working.

Some other car parts you should know about are the transmission, which transmits; the suspension, which suspends; and the pistons, which, well . . . they work real hard too.

NOW THAT YOU KNOW how cars work, you're ready to be a passenger. Every passenger has duties. Your first duty is to put on your seat belt, then we can move on to the fun stuff.

Your next duty is to test the power windows. Down. Up. Down. Partway up. Down. Up. Repeat this test every ten minutes.

Now you need to help your brother or sister stay alert. A couple of friendly pokes will do the trick, or you can start a face-making contest. Be sure to stay out of the rearview mirror visible area, so your parents can't see exactly how well you're helping with backseat alertness.

When everybody in the car gets tired of your antics, it's time to entertain people in other cars. Making googly-eyes and writing silly notes work well. It may be embarrassing, but it's your duty.

BBBB BBPP!!

EXTRA CAR NOISES FROM the BACKSEAT MAKE the CAR GO FASTER.

④ PARTWAY UP ⑤ DOWN ⑥ UP

DON'T FORGET THE WINDOWS ON THE OTHER SIDE!

DANGER ZONE
SAFE ZONE

ENTERTAINING PEOPLE IN OTHER CARS

MY FEET STINK

testing the STAIN-RESISTANT SEATS

EVERY DOG
HAS A
FAVORITE
CAR.

THE ONLY PASSENGERS who don't have duties are dogs, unless you count slobbering on the windows and shedding hair all over the seats as duties.

Dogs love to ride in cars, but what they love even more is to drive cars. When a dog chases a car down the street barking his head off, what he's saying in dog language is "Hey! Wait! Stop! I want to drive your car!" But you should never let a dog drive your car because: 1. They stop the car at every tree along the street. 2. They follow other cars too closely, so they can

*My turn!! My turn!!

ARF!!
ARF!! *

smell the other cars' behinds. However, dogs are handy to have with you in the backseat because you can blame them for all the messes, noises, and funny smells coming from back there.

Dogs Love a Drive in the Country.

SILLY DOGS!

WHEN YOU get your cut-in-half car put back together and all the passengers and dogs have done their duties, you can go on a road trip. A road trip is a way for the whole family to spend time together and annoy each other in interesting new places.

There are many wonderful places to visit on a road trip, like go-cart tracks, fudge shops, and cheap souvenir stores. Unfortunately, parents hardly ever stop at any of these places. Instead, they stop at all the historical sites. A historical site is a place where something very boring happened about a million years ago.

When you get there, your dad will find the historical marker and read out loud about some guy in 1852 who milked a cow on this very spot.

HEY DAD, STOP! DAD, STOP HERE! DAD! DAD!!

GO-CARTS

ICE CREAM

FUDGE

TAFFY

HISTORICAL MARKER

HISTORICAL DAD

DIED OF BOREDOM

Greetings from OUR BACKSEAT

MOM!! HE LOOKED AT ME!!

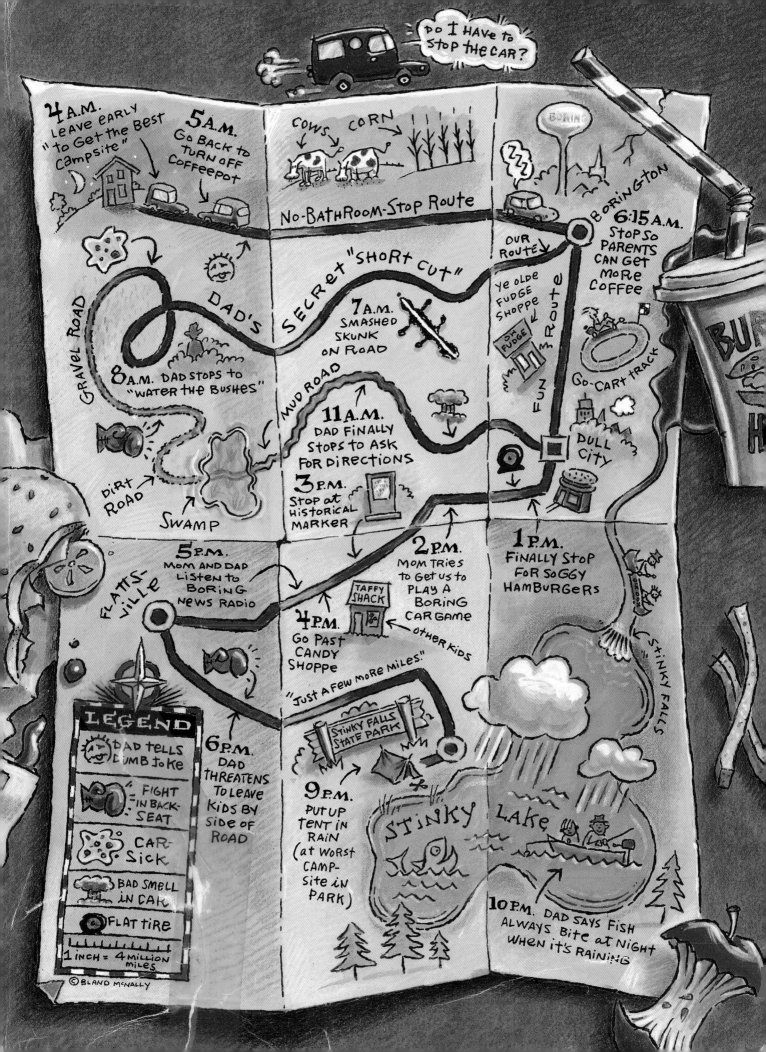

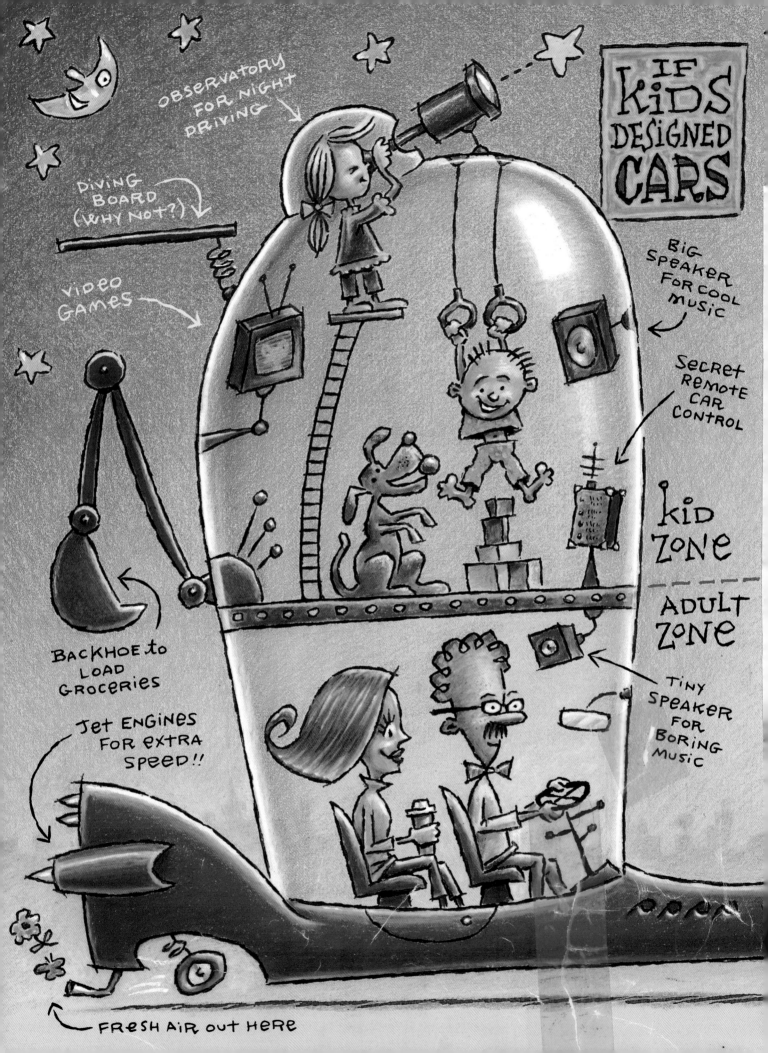

ROAD TRIPS WOULD BE MORE FUN if cars were designed by kids. First, they would have a separate play zone just for kids, and the parents would have to stay down in the adult zone listening to their boring radio shows.

Meanwhile, the kids would be upstairs, jumping around and listening to loud music. They would secretly control the car with their Secret Remote Car Control. These cars would have jet engines for extra speed and a Rocket Pod that would blast off into space when the car got into a traffic jam. Also, they would run on pollution instead of gas, and their exhaust would be fresh air, flowers, and beautiful, rare butterflies.

THE ROCKET POD BLASTS OFF!

BOOM!

CANDY STORE
TOY STORE
SKATE PARK
BEST FRIEND'S HOUSE

← SECRET REMOTE CAR CONTROL

BIG STINKY TRUCK →

POLLUTION IN HERE

ALL CARS SHOULD HAVE FLAMES

THE GIANT SLINGSHOT
HARD TO OPERATE AND NOT VERY ACCURATE: OVERALL, A BAD IDEA.

BARCO-BOARD
DAD'S FAVORITE CHAIR ATTACHED TO YOUR OLD SKATEBOARD AND THE BACK OF A CAR THAT'S GOING YOUR WAY.

ROADKILL HELMET

1. ATTACH DEAD SKUNK TO A HELMET.
2. WEAR HELMET UNTIL A BIG HAWK GRABS YOU BY THE SKUNK AND TAKES YOU AWAY.
3. ON SECOND THOUGHT, DON'T DO THIS.

the HONEY SUIT
A JUMPSUIT COATED WITH HONEY. BEES SWARM TO IT, LIFT YOU OFF THE GROUND AND FLY YOU TO THEIR HIVE. (THAT IS WHERE YOU WANTED TO GO, ISN'T IT?)

HELI-HAT
A GOOD IDEA, UNTIL IT GETS CAUGHT IN A TREE.

HUMAN CANNON
NOISY AND ONLY GOOD FOR ONE-WAY TRIPS.

EVEN THOUGH CARS are a pretty good way of getting you where you want to go, they're not perfect, so people are always trying to invent something better. These experiments are called OWGAs, which stands for Other Ways of Getting Around.

HUMAN-GAS-POWERED CAR

FIRST PLACE

BEANS

Most OWGAs sound like a good idea at first, but as you can see from these top-secret blueprints, they usually fail because of safety problems. That, or the fact that they don't take you anywhere near where you wanted to go.

Once in a while, though, someone comes up with a winner, like the human-gas-powered car, invented by Prof. Lance Flatchew.

SPECIAL ENTRANCE FOR HUMAN CANNONBALL STUDENTS

DRAG RACER

SOME PEOPLE aren't satisfied going fast while sitting on their butts; they want to go really fast while sitting on their butts. These people drive hot rods and race cars, which are faster and stinkier than regular cars.

Hot rods are old cars that have been "souped-up" with noisy engines, sparkly

Hot Rods make your HAIR BiG!

A SOUPED-UP HOT ROD

paint, and lots of shiny chrome parts. As far as I can tell, no actual soup is used in the souping-up process.

Race cars get to do all the things regular cars get in trouble for, like driving too fast, bumping into other cars, and never using their turn signals. However, since all they can do is drive around in circles, race cars are not very good at actually getting you anywhere.

ROADSTER

Fancy Italian Sports Car

Stock Car

Indy Car

Go-Carts are RACE CARS for KIDS.

THE OPPOSITE OF hot rods and race cars are earthmovers. Earthmovers include bulldozers, dump trucks, backhoes, steam shovels, and any other vehicle that's big, smelly, and yellow.

Earthmover Drivers Get to wear playclothes to work every Day!

It's fun to watch these machines at work, but you probably wonder what all this earthmoving, bulldozing, and hole digging is about. Well, as you can see on this chart, each vehicle has a specific job to do, although most of these are just excuses for digging huge holes, filling them back up, and starting all over again.

KENNY'S CONSTRUCTION COMPANY

EARTH-MOVING CHORES

NO.	VEHICLE	CHORE
1	EXCAVATOR	HELP DOG SEARCH FOR LOST BONES
2	BULLDOZER	COLLECT WORMS FOR FISHING TRIP
3	BACKHOE	SEARCH FOR PIRATE TREASURE
4	GRADER	GRADE HOMEWORK
5	CEMENT TRUCK	ROTATE CEMENT
6	LOADER	DIG SHORTCUT TO CHINA
7	DUMP TRUCKS	HAUL DIRT TO "HISTORY OF DIRT" EXHIBIT

Custom Cars

ISAVED THE MOST completely made-up cars for last. These are Custom Cars. They're made of imagination, silliness, and the occasional toilet-paper tube. They have special options you never find on normal cars, like dual water-balloon launchers or complete invisibility. The rule for inventing Custom Cars is: Go nuts!

DUAL WATER-BALLOON LAUNCHERS

Now that you know so much about cars, you can make up some of your own. To help you with the drawing part, I'll show you some of my car-drawing tricks on the next page. Pretty soon you'll be such a good car drawer that you'll get your very own Drawer's License.

OFFICIAL DRAWER'S LICENSE
THIS CERTIFIES THAT
(YOUR NAME HERE)
HAS A VIVID IMAGINATION AND A SHOEBOX FULL OF CRAYONS
Pete Casso
HEAD AR
YOUR PICTURE HERE

MAKE A COPY OF THIS and FILL IN YOUR NAME. PRESTO! YOU'RE AN Arteest !!

Once you've made up a whole bunch of cars, you'll have fun wherever you go. Because in a made-up car, getting there isn't half the fun, it's all the fun!

CARS ARE A GREAT PLACE FOR SINGING !

② ADD WHEELS

Wheels on REAL cars are perfectly round, which is boring. Wheels should have weird shapes so that your car will have a FUN, bouncy ride, kind of like bumper cars except up and down bumpy instead of sideways bumpy.

③ GIVE YOUR CAR SOME CHARACTER!

Add a DRIVER to your car. If your car is GOOFY, the driver should be GOOFY too. Instant GOOFINESS can be achieved with a BIG NOSE, a FUNNY Hat, a Silly tie, and FLAME-Red HAIR.

④ ADD some PIZAZZ!!

SHAKE LINES- a RESULT OF UNROUND WHEELS

DUST LINES- to indicate a dusty Road.

SPEED LINES- Add one line for every ten MPH.

EXHAUST SWIRLS- come in 3 types:

REGULAR	CALIFORNIA	DIESEL
eeee	...	eeee

MOTION LINES, NOT to Be CONFUSED WITH SHAKE LINES!!

TA-DA!! YOU'VE DRAWN a CAR!!

SIMON & SCHUSTER BOOKS *for* YOUNG READERS

An imprint of Simon & Schuster Children's Publishing Division
1230 Avenue of the Americas, New York, New York 10020

SIMON & SCHUSTER BOOKS FOR YOUNG READERS
is a trademark of Simon & Schuster, Inc.

Book design by Tom Lichtenheld

Dedication page illustration by Jack Lichtenheld

The text for this book is set in Biffin, tweaked by Bob Blewett.

The illustrations are rendered in ink, colored pencil,
gouache, watercolor, and 10w40.

Manufactured in China

10 9 8 7 6 5 4 3 2 1 blastoff!

Library of Congress Cataloging-in-Publication Data
Lichtenheld, Tom.
Everything I know about cars / Tom Lichtenheld. 1st ed.
p. cm.
ISBN 0-689-84382-8
1. Automobiles—Juvenile literature. I. Title.
TL206.L53 2005
388.3'42—dc22   2004041623

The End

My dad drew this cartoon when I was a kid, and I never forgot it.
I owe my bouncy cars, and much else, to him.

For my parents, Jack and Scotti, who surrounded me with humor and art.

With gratitude to my wife, coach, and collaborator, Jan Miller.